Cinderella

Including The Princess and The Frog & Rapunzel

igloobooks

Cinderella

There once lived a man who had a kind and pretty wife and a beautiful daughter. Sadly, the man's wife died soon after their daughter was born. A few years later, the man married again. His second wife was not kind and pretty, and she already had two daughters who were so selfish, proud and greedy that they were known as the "ugly sisters". From the first day they moved in, the ugly sisters were cruel and unkind to their stepsister. They made Cinderella clean the house from top to bottom, do all the cooking and clear out the cinders from the fireplace. She spent so much time doing this that her stepsisters called her "Cinderella".

One day, the King and Queen decided to hold a grand ball. The two ugly sisters couldn't believe their luck when, the very next day, an invitation arrived. On the night of the ball, the ugly sisters paraded their new clothes in front of poor Cinderella and asked her to tell them what suited them best.

After they'd left, Cinderella sat on the little stool near the fire. "Why are my sisters so cruel to me?" she thought. "I do everything they tell me to do around the house, and more! They never give me a kind word, or even smile at me." She felt so unhappy she began to cry.

Suddenly, a beautiful woman, carrying a silver wand, appeared right in front of her. She seemed to have come from nowhere.
"Who are you?" gasped Cinderella, a little frightened.
"Don't be scared. I am your Fairy Godmother," said the beautiful woman. "What's the matter, child? Why are you crying?"
"I would have loved to have gone to the ball," wept Cinderella. "But my stepsisters don't want me to go. "Don't worry," said her Fairy Godmother, kindly. You shall go to the ball! But, first, I'd like you to bring me some things. I need a pumpkin, two mice and the biggest rat you can find."With one wave of her silver wand, the Fairy Godmother changed the pumpkin into a golden coach, the mice into two magnificent white horses and the rat into a coachman.

With another wave of her wand, the Fairy Godmother changed Cinderella's ragged dress into a ball gown made of the finest satin and silver thread. On her feet were a pair of beautiful glass slippers.
"Now, go and enjoy yourself," said the Fairy Godmother. "But be sure to be back before midnight, for when the clock strikes twelve everything will return to what it was before."
Cinderella stepped into the glistening carriage and was whisked through the dark streets until she reached the palace.

When she entered the ballroom, everyone stared. They had never seen such a beautiful girl before. The Prince fell in love with her as soon as he saw her, and danced with her all evening. She was having such a wonderful time, she forgot all about her Fairy Godmother's warning. All of a sudden, she heard the clock strike twelve.

"Oh, no," she thought, "I must leave!"
She tore herself from the Prince's arms and rushed out of the ballroom.

The Prince couldn't understand why this lovely girl had suddenly run away. He searched the Palace for her, but couldn't find her anywhere. But, in her rush to leave, Cinderella had left behind one of her glass slippers. When the Prince found it on the Palace steps, he immediately said that he intended to find and marry the girl whose foot fitted the glass slipper. He would visit every house in the land, until he had found her.

The ugly sisters became very excited. On the day that the Prince was going to visit their house, they made sure to wear their best dresses.

When the Prince arrived, he held out the glass slipper and asked which one of the sisters would like to try it on first.
"I will!" cried one of them. But, as much as she tried to push and, squeeze her foot into the slipper, it just wouldn't fit. Her foot was far too big.

"Give it to me!" said the other sister and, grabbing the slipper, tried to put it on. But her foot was far too big, too. However much she pushed and tugged, she just couldn't get her foot into it.

Just then, Cinderella stepped forward. She had been standing quietly in the shadows and no one had noticed her.

"May I try?" she asked, shyly. "You!" cried the ugly sisters. "Of course you can't! Now get back to the kitchen where you belong!"

"Be quiet!" ordered the Prince. "Of course you may," he said, turning to Cinderella, not recognizing her. Cinderella sat down and put the slipper onto her foot. It glided on perfectly. The ugly sisters gasped in amazement. "I recognize you now," said the Prince, smiling. "You are the girl I fell in love with at the ball, and you are the girl I am going to marry." Cinderella replied "I loved you the moment I met you." Cinderella and the Prince had a glorious wedding. She forgave her sisters and never had to wash up a dirty dish ever again.

The Princess and The Frog

Long, long ago, there was a King who had three lovely
daughters who all lived together in a magnificent castle. The
King's youngest daughter liked the simple things in life. She
enjoyed walking in the castle grounds, humming songs to herself. She
loved the sweet scent of the flowers and watching all the little animals
scurrying around the woods.

One day, the Princess found herself at the furthest point of the castle
grounds. Here stood an old well that had not been used for many years.
The Princess sat on the edge of the well and started to throw a small
golden ball in the air. She caught it and threw it up again, this time a
little higher. The next time she caught it, she threw it higher still. But
the next time, the ball went so high she couldn't catch it at all, and it fell
all the way down into the murky waters of the well.
"I've had that ball ever since I was a baby," thought the Princess. She
was so upset at losing her precious golden ball, she began to cry.
"I'll get it back for you," she heard a voice say.
The Princess stopped crying and looked around but couldn't see
anyone.
"I wonder where that voice came from," she thought.
"I'm here," said the voice.
The Princess looked down and saw that the voice belonged to a frog
that was staring up at her.
"But you're a frog!" exclaimed the astonished Princess.

"I am a frog, and I will get your ball back on the condition that you look after me. You must take me back to the castle with you. You must play with me, allow me to eat from your plate at the table and let me sleep in your bed. If you agree to all this, I will bring your ball back."

The Princess hated the idea of spending so much time with a slimy frog. But she wanted her golden ball back so much that she agreed to his conditions at once. The frog dived into the well and, shortly after, reappeared with the ball in his mouth. The Princess took the ball from him and ran back to the castle as fast as she could.

That evening, the Princess and her sisters were sitting with their father
having their dinner when she heard a little scratching noise at the door.
She opened the door but there was no one there. Then she heard a little
croak at her feet. She looked down and saw the frog staring up at her .
"Oh, no!" thought the Princess. "He's found me!"
"Hello, Princess," said the frog. "That wasn't very nice, running away
from me like that. Here I am to make sure you keep your promise."

"What is the meaning of all this?" asked the King, a little harshly.

"I lost my ball down the well," began the Princess. "This frog got it back for me and, in return, I promised to look after him. But I don't want to!"

"I see," said the King, stroking his beard, thoughtfully. "I'm sorry, my dear, but a promise must be kept. I'm afraid that you must look after our little friend for as long as he wishes."

"Very well, father," answered the Princess meekly and sat back down at the table. So the poor Princess had to feed the frog all evening, and found it so disgusting that she completely lost her appetite.

At the end of dinner, the Princess got down from her chair and stomped up the stairs to her bedroom.

"I'm a bit tired, too," yawned the frog who, after bidding good night to the King and the Princess's sisters, hopped across the room and followed the Princess up the stairs.

In her bedroom, the Princess quickly got into her nightgown, brushed her teeth and jumped into bed. Out of the corner of her eye, she'd noticed that the frog had come into the room and was crouching quietly in the corner. "And you can sleep right where you are!" she yelled at him. "I don't want your ugly body anywhere near me!"

"You know, there is one way you can be rid of me," said the frog, jumping into bed beside her. "If you were to give me one kiss on my lips I would leave here immediately and never return."
"That's the most horrible thing I've ever heard of!" cried the Princess. "Your lips are so slimy!"
"Well, it's up to you," said the frog. "But remember, you'd never see me again." The Princess realized that if she wanted to be rid of the frog, she'd just have to overcome her disgust and kiss his green, slippery mouth. She shut her eyes and kissed the frog's lips as quickly as she could.

All at once, there was a sudden blinding flash and to the Princess's utter astonishment the frog had completely disappeared and in its place stood a young, handsome Prince. The Prince explained that a wicked witch had cast a spell on him many years before that had turned him into a frog and the only person who could break the spell would be a young, lovely Princess who would kiss him on the lips.

The Prince and Princess got married and the Prince took his new bride to live in his own land. Everyone at his castle welcomed him home, happy to see the return of their Prince whom they'd thought was lost to them forever.

Rapunzel

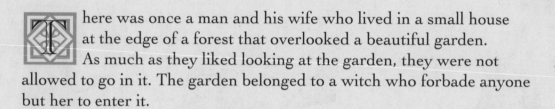

There was once a man and his wife who lived in a small house at the edge of a forest that overlooked a beautiful garden. As much as they liked looking at the garden, they were not allowed to go in it. The garden belonged to a witch who forbade anyone but her to enter it.

One day, the man's wife announced to her husband that she was going to have a baby. Not long after, she became very ill. She lay in bed, refused to eat and got thinner and thinner.

"There's only one thing that can help me," she told her husband "There is a strange herb growing in the witch's garden, called rapunzel. If you can get some for me, it will make me well again."

That night, the man quietly tiptoed into the garden and made his way to where the rapunzel herb grew. He bent down and started to pick the ripe, green leaves.
"How dare you steal my herbs!" a voice suddenly rang out. It was the witch, who stood towering over the poor man with an evil look on her face. "I didn't mean any harm." he stammered but my wife is very ill and the only thing that will make her better are the leaves of the rapunzel herb."

"I see," said the witch, thinking for a moment. "All right," she finally said. "You may take as much rapunzel as you wish, but only on the condition that when your child is born, you must hand the infant over to me." It was a difficult choice to make but, fearing that his wife might die, the poor man agreed to the witch's demand.

After eating the rapunzel leaves, the man's wife did get well again and a few months later, she gave birth to a beautiful baby girl. No sooner had the couple wrapped their child in a blanket than the witch appeared to claim her prize. "I believe this child is mine. I think I'll call her Rapunzel, after the herb that you stole from my garden," she cackled loudly. She grabbed the baby from her mother's arms and whisked her away into the forest.

As Rapunzel grew up, the witch made sure she neither saw nor spoke to any other living person. Fearing that she might try to escape, the witch put Rapunzel at the top of a tall tower that lay deep in the forest. There were no stairs, only one small window and no door.

Rapunzel had never had her beautiful hair cut, so her hair was thick, golden and very, very long. Once a day, the witch delivered Rapunzel's food. She'd stand at the bottom of the tower and call up. "Rapunzel, Rapunzel! Let down your golden hair." Rapunzel would throw down her plaited hair that reached right to the bottom of the tower. Then the witch would climb steadily up. After the witch had delivered her food, she climbed down the same golden rope.

One day, a young Prince was riding through the forest. As he rode, he heard someone singing nearby. The voice was so lovely, he decided to find out where it came from. It seemed to be coming from a tall tower nearby. The Prince got off his horse and looked for a door, but couldn't find an enterance.

Just then he heard footsteps behind him. He hid behind a bush and saw a witch walking towards the tower with a tray of food. She called out, climbed up, climbed down again then disappeared into the forest.

"So, that's the way in," thought the Prince. He went to the foot of the tower and called up. "Rapunzel, Rapunzel! Let down your golden hair." The hair came cascading down and the Prince began to climb up. When he reached the top, he saw Rapunzel and thought she was the most beautiful girl he'd ever seen. They liked each other very much and talked for hours.